Paul Bunyan

Tale retold by Bill Balcziak
Illustrated by Patrick Girouard

Adviser: Dr. Alexa Sandmann, Professor of Literacy,
The University of Toledo; Member, International Reading Association

COMPASS POINT BOOKS
Minneapolis, Minnesota

Compass Point Books
3109 West 50th Street, #115
Minneapolis, MN 55410

Visit Compass Point Books on the Internet at *www.compasspointbooks.com*
or e-mail your request to *custserv@compasspointbooks.com*

Photograph ©: Jim Wark, 28.

Editor: Catherine Neitge
Designer: Les Tranby

Library of Congress Cataloging-in-Publication Data
Balcziak, Bill, 1962-
 Paul Bunyan / written by Bill Balcziak; illustrated by Patrick Girouard.
  p. cm.— (The Imagination Series: Tall tales)
Summary: Presents the life story of the enormous lumberjack, Paul Bunyan, who along with his blue ox Babe,
is said to have made the 10,000 lakes of Minnesota with his footsteps.
 ISBN 0-7565-0459-7 (hardcover)
 1. Bunyan, Paul (Legendary character)—Legends. [1. Bunyan, Paul (Legendary character)—Legends.
 2. Folklore—United States. 3. Tall tales.] I. Title. II. Series.
 PZ8.1.B183 Pau 2003
 398.2'0973'02—dc21   2002015118

Table of Contents

Giant of a Man

It started with some shaking on the forest floor. Squirrels and birds raced for cover. There was a rumble. Then there was a loud bang and a big boom. Trees swayed and danced. Was it a mighty thunderstorm? The once quiet forest was alive with noise. Then, as quickly as it began, the noise stopped. The forest grew quiet.

An enormous man stood in a clearing near a large pond. He was taller than the treetops. His shoulders were as wide as a house. He wore a red flannel shirt and sturdy pants, like the kind worn by lumberjacks. He carried an ax with a handle as long as a pine tree. His big muscles made it clear he could swing the ax very hard. He looked hot and tired, as though he had been working all day.

The man kneeled down and slid his huge hand into the pond. He scooped up some water and drank. "Now that," said the giant, "is the best water I have ever tasted!" He rose up, stretched his arms wide, and turned toward the setting sun. With another explosion of noise, he crashed away through the woods. Just like that, he was gone. The forest grew silent once again.

The legend of Paul Bunyan started in the north woods more than a century ago. Today, nearly everyone knows about this giant, whose adventures took him across North America. The tales about Paul Bunyan are almost as "tall" as the man himself.

Big Baby Bunyan

Not surprisingly, Paul Bunyan started life as a very, very big baby. How big? It took six strong storks to carry him to his new parents' home in Maine. When he arrived, his mother wept with joy. She loved her big, strong, beautiful baby. When she tried to take him in her arms, however, he weighed so much that she sank in the ground all the way up to her waist.

Baby Paul was always hungry, and he let people know it. He cried so loudly, the sound cracked a man's eyeglasses five miles away.

Paul's mother fed him:
- Ten gallons of milk
- Twenty pancakes
- Thirty pints of berries (He cried for more!)
- Forty pounds of oatmeal
- Fifty slices of bread
- Sixty strips of bacon
- Seventy sausages
- Eighty eggs
- Ninety crackers
- One hundred spoonfuls of applesauce

That was just his breakfast!

Oh, how that baby grew! When the storks brought him, he wore a diaper made from a potato sack. After a week, he outgrew his father's clothes. Within a month, his mother sewed his pants out of blankets and his shirts out of tents.

Little Paul slept in a crib made from a hay wagon. He was rocked to sleep by a team of horses pulling on either side.

One morning Paul slipped out of his crib and rolled down a big hill to the ocean. He tumbled right in. His splashing caused the tide to rise WAY above normal.

By the time his parents dragged him to shore, boats were sunk all along the coast. Villages were flooded, and people were mad! Angry villagers told the Bunyans to raise their big baby someplace else.

11

Look at Him Grow

So the Bunyans moved. They made a raft of pine trees and sailed young Paul all the way up the Saint Lawrence River.

People from all around came to see the Bunyan lad grow. "Oh my," they would exclaim, "that boy is mighty big!" By age four, he could reach the tops of small trees. By age six, he was as tall as an oak. At age ten, he stood twice as high as a white pine.

One day, his father decided to build a house closer to the lake.

"Father," Paul said, "why not just move our house rather than build a new one?"

His father shook his head. "It would take a team of forty horses working all day to drag that house to a new spot," he said.

Paul laughed with glee. He reached down and picked up his parents' house in his chubby hands. He carried it more than a mile to a nice, shady place by the water. "There, Father," he said. "Is that a good spot?" His father beamed with pride.

Of course, young Paul was too big to sleep in the house. His father made him a special bed in a large barn nearby. He filled the barn with straw to keep the boy warm during the cold winter nights.

When Paul was twelve, the winter was the coldest anybody had ever seen. Birds froze in midair and stayed there until the spring thaw. People's breath hung in solid, frozen clouds that bumped

their heads if they weren't careful.

   One night it got so cold the falling snow turned from white to blue. Blue icicles as big as logs hung everywhere. Blue snow formed huge drifts. The night sky glowed with the color of the snow and the ice and the clouds.

During the night, Paul heard a terrible noise. It sounded like a train—maybe an express—but Paul knew there were no trains running on *this* night. He opened the barn door and stared into the blizzard. He couldn't see anything. "It must be the wind," Paul said to himself. He went back to sleep and tried to keep warm.

The next morning, he bundled up and went outside. The whole world was blue. He walked toward the lake and stopped in front of a huge pile of snow. The strange noise was coming from inside.

Paul started digging. To his surprise, a large brown eye looked up at him through the hole. It blinked. Paul cleared more blue snow. Now he could see two eyes. He dug some more. A pair of horns appeared.

Babe, the Blue Ox

"It's an ox!" Paul cried. The animal climbed out of the snow, and even Paul was shocked at its size. The ox stood 24 ax handles tall and had strong, wide shoulders.

The poor beast was so cold it had turned as blue as the snow. It cried, and Paul remembered the sound of a train the night before. He covered his ears against the roar.

Paul leaned down to warm the beast. He was surprised when it nuzzled its snout into his arms. After the creature warmed up, Paul stepped back and stared. The ox was still blue! "You're a special animal," said Paul with a smile.

He called the ox "Babe" and they became the very best of friends. No matter where Paul Bunyan's adventures took him, Babe, the Blue Ox, was with him every giant step of the way.

When Paul turned 18, his father made him an ax from the trunk of an ash. The ax head was forged from metal melted down from an old steam engine. "Son," said Mr. Bunyan, "it is time for you to make your way in the world. Go west, and find work in the lumber camps."

Paul and Babe were sad to leave Ma and Pa Bunyan but excited to start a new adventure. Paul tipped his cap to his father and lifted his mother up for a hug. "Paul Bunyan! You put me down right now, you hear?" his mother cried from amid the treetops. But she smiled as she said it.

No sooner had Paul started his journey than he heard gold had been discovered in nearby Michigan! Paul and Babe raced to get there only to find great forests where the gold was supposed to be.

"I'll be hornswoggled," said Paul. Babe snorted.

"Well," said Paul, after they made camp, "let's start looking for that gold." With a single swing of his giant ax, Paul cleared a HUGE area. Soon, thousands of trees had been cleared. There was still no sign of gold.

"I guess we'll just start digging

for the gold, then," he sighed. Paul hitched a plow to Babe and the ox dug in and began to pull. "Pull harder, Babe! Pull!" Paul shouted.

Soon, Babe had dug five huge holes. There was still no gold. Paul and Babe were sad. They left the area and continued their journey west. When the rains came that summer, the five holes filled with water. They became what we now call the Great Lakes!

Life as a Lumberjack

Paul and Babe settled in Minnesota where Paul ran a lumber camp. It was the biggest camp in the world. The people who worked there had to be *at least* ten feet (three meters) tall. To prove their strength, they had to lift a felled tree over their heads while standing on Babe's shoulders.

The lumberjacks worked hard every day. In the evenings they liked to sit around the fire and eat and drink their fill. Paul hired a cook named Sourdough Sam to prepare meals for the crew. Sam used an enormous griddle to make his famous flapjacks.

To grease the griddle, the lumberjacks tied hunks of bacon to their boots and skated around until the grease was bubbling hot. In addition, it took a dozen loggers working nonstop to cut enough wood to keep the fire going. Sourdough Sam would yell "Hurry, now! Hurry! The fire's about out!" and the workers would throw more logs on the fire.

That first Minnesota winter was hard on the loggers. The snow was so deep they had to dig *down* to find the trees. When the spring melt came, the crew floated the logs downstream on the river current. The Mississippi River had so many turns, however, the logs jammed up.

"I can fix that," said Paul with a wink. "Come on Babe!" Paul tied the end of the river to Babe's tail. The big ox pulled the river until it was completely straight. It stayed straight just long enough for the logs to arrive safely downstream.

Today, when a thunderstorm

rolls through the north woods, people go to their windows hoping to spot Paul Bunyan crashing through the forest. But he's rarely seen anymore. Still, people continue to share many stories about his adventures.

Can't you just imagine how Paul's footprints made each of Minnesota's 10,000 lakes? Isn't it interesting to think of Babe slipping on some ice and skidding across the Dakota Territory? Now you know why the plains are completely flat and treeless! Could it be true?

Or is it a tall tale?

The many lakes of the Boundary Waters lie on Minnesota's border with Canada.

A Wild Old Tale

The legend of Paul Bunyan is one of the oldest and wildest of all the tall tales. Many people believe the tale started in the logging camps of Canada in the 1800s. At that time, loggers spent long, hard winters working in the camps. At night, they would gather around the fire and tell stories. Each man tried to top the last story.

The story of Paul Bunyan may have begun as a true story about an extremely large lumberjack. Over time, and in the course of many stories, Paul Bunyan became the biggest of all the tall tale legends. Eventually, the story made it into a newspaper and Paul Bunyan and Babe, the Blue Ox, became famous around the world.

North Woods Pancakes

Brrrrrrr! It gets cold in the north woods of Minnesota, Michigan, and Maine. A good breakfast helps you keep warm. Here is a recipe for pancakes that Paul would love! It makes eight servings.

1 1/2 cups all-purpose flour
3 1/2 teaspoons baking powder
1 teaspoon salt
1 tablespoon sugar

1 1/4 cups milk
1 egg
3 tablespoons butter, melted

In a large bowl, sift together the flour, baking powder, salt, and sugar. In a smaller bowl, mix together the milk, egg, and melted butter. Make a well in the center of the dry ingredients and pour in the milk mixture, stirring until smooth. Have an adult help you heat a lightly oiled griddle or frying pan over medium high heat. Pour the batter onto the griddle, using about 1/4 cup for each pancake. Brown on both sides and serve hot with butter and syrup.

Glossary

amazement—great surprise or wonder

blizzard—a large snowstorm

enormous—very large

express—a fast train that makes few stops

felled—a tree that has been cut down

flannel—wool or cotton cloth often used to make work shirts

forge—to form something from metal using heat or a hammer

Great Lakes—a group of five connected freshwater lakes that lie along the border between the United States and Canada; they are Lakes Superior, Michigan, Huron, Erie, and Ontario

hornswoggled—slang for tricked by underhanded methods

legend—a story passed down through the years that may not be completely true

muscles—the parts of the body that help you move, lift, or push

rumble—a noise like the sound of thunder

Saint Lawrence River—a river that runs in North America from the Great Lakes to the Atlantic Ocean

thaw—weather that is warm enough to melt snow and ice

Did You Know?

✗ The first printed Paul Bunyan story appeared in the *Detroit News-Tribune* on July 24, 1910.

✗ There are more than 200 roadside statues of Paul Bunyan in the United States.

✗ A giant statue of Paul Bunyan was built for the Chicago Railroad Fair in 1948. It now stands in Brainerd, Minnesota.

✗ Paul Bunyan appeared on a 32-cent United States postage stamp in 1996.

Want to Know More?

At the Library

Jensen, Patsy and Jean Pidgeon. *Paul Bunyan and His Blue Ox.* New York: Troll Communications, 1997.

Kellogg, Steven. *Paul Bunyan.* New York: William Morrow and Co., 1985.

Osborne, Mary Pope. *American Tall Tales.* New York: Scholastic, 1991.

Spies, Karen. *Our Folk Heroes.* Brookfield, Conn.: The Millbrook Press, 1994.

Walker, Paul Robert. *Big Men, Big Country: A Collection of American Tall Tales.* New York: Harcourt, 1999.

On the Web

Lumbering in Michigan
http://www.michiganhistory.org/museum/explore/museums/hismus/prehist/lumber/index.html
To tour the lumbering gallery at the Michigan State Historical Society

Tic-Tac-Toe
http://www.paulbunyantrail.com/game.html
To play tic-tac-toe with Babe, the Blue Ox

The Paul Bunyan Trail
http://www.paulbunyantrail.com/
To learn about a huge recreational trail project in northern Minnesota named after the legendary Paul Bunyan

Through the Mail

Bemidji: The Home of Paul Bunyan
Bemidji Visitors & Convention Bureau
P.O. Box 66
Bemidji, MN 56619
800/458-2223 Ext. 105
To write for information about Paul Bunyan and Babe, the Blue Ox

On the Road

Paul Bunyan Logging Camp
110 Carson Park Drive
Eau Claire, WI 54702-0221
715/835-6200
To visit an interpretive center with an interactive tall tales room and other buildings authentic to the 1900s logging era

Index

About the Author
Bill Balcziak has written a number of books for children. When he is not writing, he enjoys going to plays, movies, and museums. Bill lives in Minnesota with his family under the shadow of Paul Bunyan and Babe, the Blue Ox.

About the Illustrator
Patrick Girouard has been drawing and painting for many years. He has illustrated more than fifty books for children. Patrick has two sons, Marc and Max, and a dog called Sam. They all live in Indiana.

Everything you want to know about
Creepy Crawlies

Contents

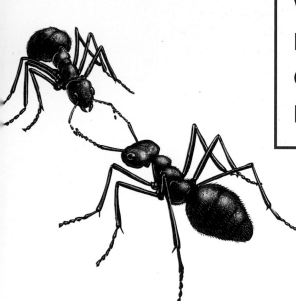

TS

Staying Small

Creepy crawlies—insects, spiders, and other minibeasts—are small compared with most other animals. There are lots of reasons for this. Creepy crawlies don't have backbones to support their bodies, like humans do. So the bodies of many minibeasts are covered by a hard outer casing that acts like an outside skeleton, to support and protect the animal. If a bug got too big, this casing would become too heavy for it to move. Also, bugs don't have lungs. They breathe through air tubes that go from the surface of the body to the inside. If these tubes were too long, fresh air would not flow in fast enough. A giant bug would have difficulty breathing. There are also many advantages to being small.

What is the smallest insect?

One of the tiniest insects is the fairy fly wasp. It is so small that it would fit inside this "o." It looks more like a fly than a wasp. Being this small does have some problems. A fairy fly wasp can't fight its enemies— they're all bigger than it is. But it can hide in tiny cracks where predators can't reach!

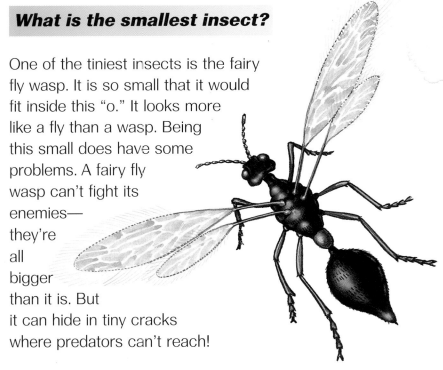

Why is it better to be small?

One reason that bugs stay small is so that they can move around easily to find food. They also need less food than large animals. This means lots of creepy crawlies can live together in one place. This makes finding a mate and breeding easier, too. Midges are tiny flies. Thousands of them fly in a swarm, courting and mating in midair. Some feed on plant juices but others bite animals and suck their blood. They'll even have a meal on you if they get the chance!

Were there prehistoric creepy crawlies?

Yes, the first creepy crawlies left the seas to live on land about 500 million years ago, long before dinosaurs even existed. *Meganeura*, a huge dragonfly, lived 270 million years ago. It hunted other flying bugs for food.

Arthropleura was a giant 6-foot-long, armored millipede. It also lived about 270 million years ago and was one of the biggest creepy crawlies ever to walk on Earth.

Which is the heaviest insect?

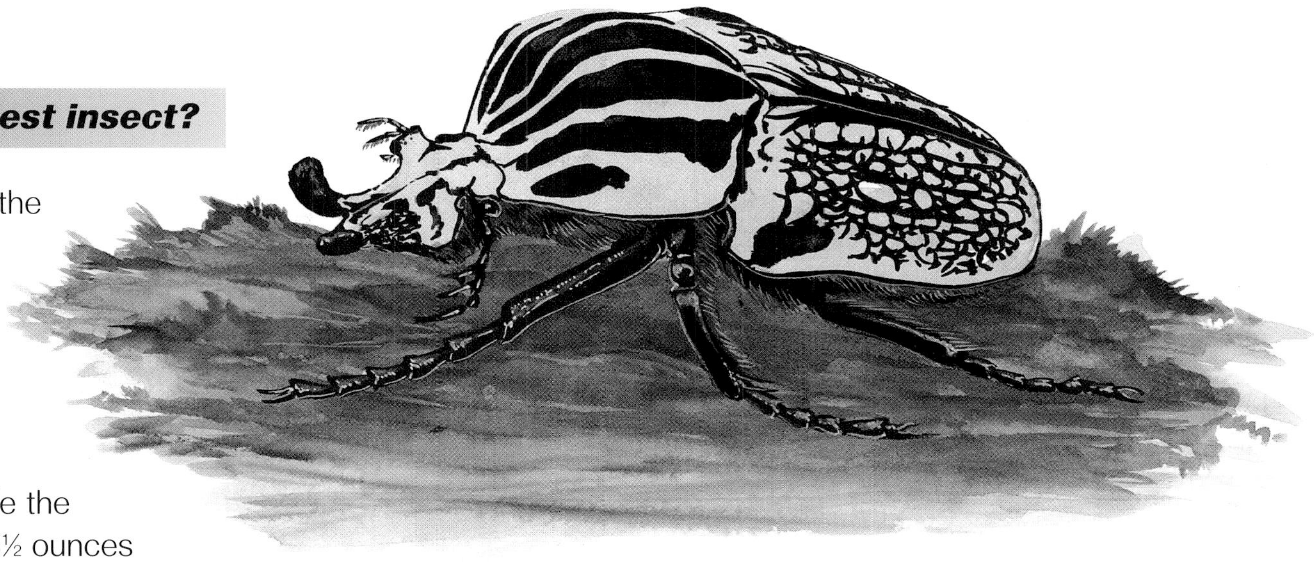

The Goliath beetle from the tropical rain forests of Africa is about 4¼ inches long. That's about as big as an insect can grow. Its thick outer casing is like armor, making the Goliath beetle the heaviest insect at over 3½ ounces (about the weight of an apple). If it were any larger, the Goliath beetle wouldn't be able to move.

Do adult moths and butterflies grow?

No, adult moths and butterflies do all their growing when they are caterpillars. As a caterpillar grows, it sheds its skin. The soft skin underneath, which fits its new, bigger body, slowly hardens. It may shed its skin several times before it is fully grown. The elephant hawk moth is one of the largest flying insects. Each of its wings is almost 2¾ inches across—that's about the width of your hand.

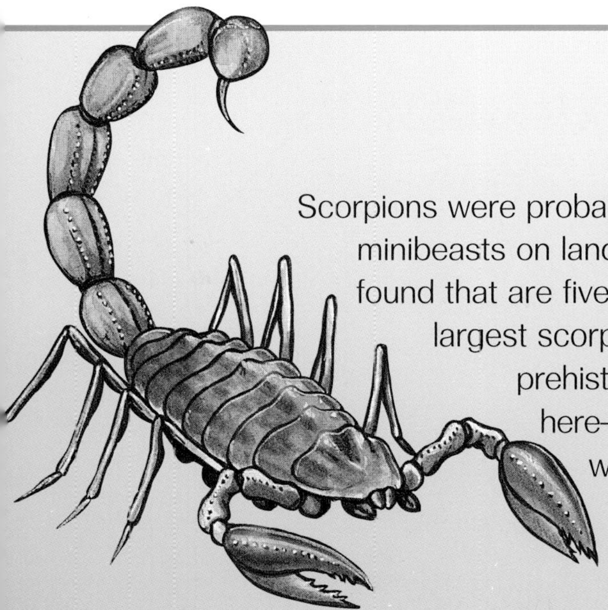

Do bugs live on each other?

Yes, bugs like these tiny mites can live almost anywhere. Mites have eight legs and belong to the same group of animals as spiders. There are thousands of different kinds of mite. Some stab plant stems and suck up the juices, called sap. Others live and feed on animals, biting them and sucking up their blood. The two red mites here are small enough to hitch a ride on a spider's leg.

Scorpions were probably some of the first minibeasts on land. Fossils have been found that are five times as big as the largest scorpion alive today. This prehistoric scorpion shown here—*Gigantoscorpion*—was 23½ inches long.

The first spiders lived about 370 million years ago. *Arthrolycosa* was a large spider with long legs. It had special fangs that it probably used to poison its prey.

Bug-eyed!

Minibeasts come in many shapes and varieties and so do their eyes. Some creepy crawlies have simple eyes that can only tell light from dark. Most insects are "bug-eyed." They see the world as a jigsaw of tiny pictures. An insect's eyes are made up of lots of little lenses. Each lens produces a tiny part of the overall picture. Spiders have two, four, six, or eight eyes to spot their prey very quickly. Other bugs have no eyes at all. They live underground, or in caves or deep water, where there is little or no light. Without light, you cannot see, so eyes are useless.

Can spiders see well?

Yes, most spiders can. Simple eyes around the head help them spot their prey very quickly. The zebra jumping spider has eight simple eyes of various sizes. Three pairs of eyes on the sides of its head help the spider spot an animal moving nearby. Then it stalks its prey using its main, central eyes, which give a clearer view. It judges how far away its meal is, then jumps for the kill!

Where are a snail's eyes?

Snails, like this giant African land snail, have eyes on the tips of their tentacles. Eyes on stalks can be very useful. The snail can extend its tentacles to have a good look around, then pull them back into its head for safety. A snail's eyes cannot see any details, only blurred patches of light and dark. But that's enough for this giant snail—the biggest in the world—to find its food. It gobbles up crops, dead animals, and even other snails.

Do insects have noses to smell with?

Insects can smell, but they do not have noses. They pick up smells with their feelers, or antennae. Ants use feelers to sniff out food, find their nest and to tell friends from enemies.

Many male moths have large feathery feelers to pick up smells. Male emperor moths can smell females up to 7 miles away! Most female moths have smoother antennae.

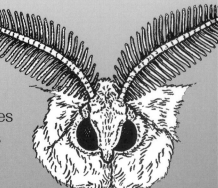

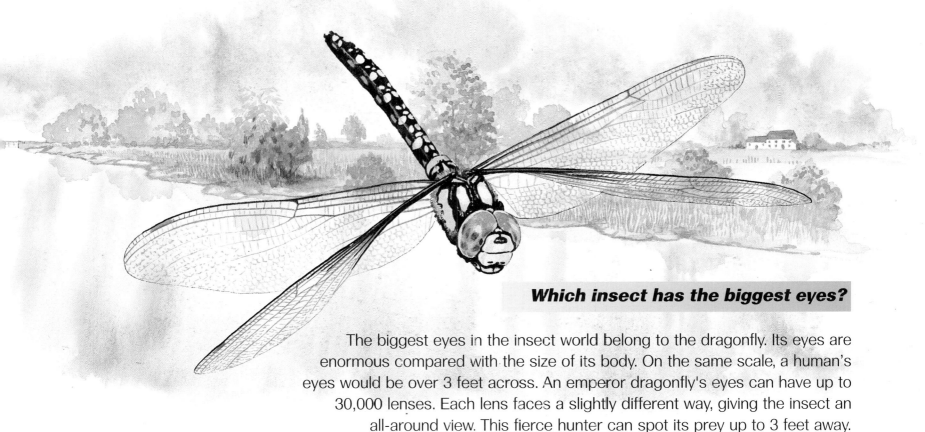

Which insect has the biggest eyes?

The biggest eyes in the insect world belong to the dragonfly. Its eyes are enormous compared with the size of its body. On the same scale, a human's eyes would be over 3 feet across. An emperor dragonfly's eyes can have up to 30,000 lenses. Each lens faces a slightly different way, giving the insect an all-around view. This fierce hunter can spot its prey up to 3 feet away.

Can worms see?

Proper eyes would not be much use beneath the ground, so an earthworm doesn't have any. However, patches of skin on the upper part of its head can tell light from dark. These warn the earthworm when it is near to the surface. This giant Australian earthworm is a real monster. It is thicker than a thumb, grows up to 12 feet long and squirts a foul-smelling liquid at its enemies!

Which bug can see in air and under water?

Have you ever tried seeing under water? If you have, you will know that things look blurred. This is because our eyes are made to see in air. The whirligig beetle spends its life swimming round and round on the surface of a pond. It can see in both air and water. How does it do it? Simple! Its eyes are divided into two parts. The top halves look into the air above the surface of the pond. The bottom halves look down into the water.

Butterflies have antennae shaped like tiny clubs. They use them to sniff out food plants. But they don't use their antennae for tasting. They check whether food tastes good with their feet!

The long-horned beetle gets its name from its extra-long antennae. The male beetle's antennae help him sniff out a mate from several miles away.

7

All Change

Human babies look like little adults, but many baby bugs don't look anything like their parents. As some bugs grow up, their bodies change shape. This means that they lead different kinds of lives at each stage. Insects start life as tiny eggs. An egg hatches into the next stage—a larva. Larvae spend nearly all their lives eating, growing, shedding their skins (molting), and then eating some more. Some larvae, like fly maggots, look very different from their parents. They change their shape again to become adults. Other types of bug larvae, such as baby crickets, look more like their parents.

What do baby flies look like?

Adult shield bug

Baby flies are white wiggly larvae, usually called maggots. These greenbottle larvae look nothing like their parents. They do nothing but eat moldy meat, molt, and grow. Each larva then turns into a pupa—a hard, protective case with the larva inside. The body of the larva breaks down and changes into an adult. When the pupa breaks open, the fly crawls out and flies off.

Which baby insects look like their parents?

Many baby insects, such as shield bugs, grasshoppers, and crickets, look quite like mini-adults. These babies are called nymphs. Shield bug nymphs, however, have no wings. As the nymph grows, it sheds its hard skin. The new skin is soft and allows the body to grow before the skin hardens again. Each time it molts, a nymph grows more like an adult.

Shield bug nymphs

What do baby bugs eat?

The brown hawker dragonfly nymph lives in water. It creeps toward its prey, then shoots forward a hinged flap, or mask. The mask has needle-sharp fangs for stabbing.

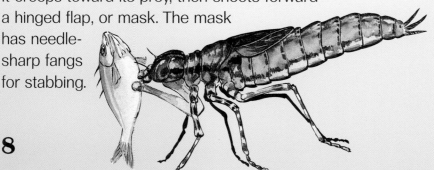

Honeybee larvae are especially lucky. Worker bees in the hive collect nectar and pollen each day. This is used to make the sweet honey that the larvae are fed on.

How do caterpillars turn into butterflies?

These pictures show the stages in the life of a swallowtail butterfly.
1. The adult butterfly lays her eggs on a leaf. The egg is the first stage of a butterfly's life.
2. The egg hatches into a caterpillar, or larva. The caterpillar spends its life eating leaves. It eats, molts, and grows. The young caterpillar changes its shape and color as it grows.

1. Egg

2. Young caterpillar

Older caterpillar

3. In butterflies and moths, the caterpillar turns into a pupa, or chrysalis. Inside the hard case, the body parts move around and change shape.
4. The chrysalis splits open and the adult butterfly crawls out. It spreads its wings to dry, then flies off to find a mate. This complete change of body shape is called metamorphosis.

4. Adult butterfly

3. Pupa or chrysalis

Other insects that go through these four stages include moths, beetles, flies, bees, wasps, and ants.

The great diving beetle larva lives in fresh water. It stabs small animals like tadpoles with its fangs and injects its prey with juices. These break down the body into a thick soup.

The codling moth larva has strong, sharp jaws. But it doesn't use them to slice up meat. Instead, this hungry caterpillar scrunches its way through even the hardest apples.

On the Move

Since life began on Earth, millions of years ago, many kinds of minibeast have developed. They all have different body shapes, and different types and numbers of legs. Each group of animals is suited to the place it lives in and the kind of life it leads. Insects, such as flies, have six legs. Arachnids, such as spiders, have eight legs. Centipedes and millipedes have lots of legs. Slugs, worms, and snails have none!

How many legs do insects have?

All insects have six legs, but they come in many shapes and sizes. Legs also have many different uses. This is a creosote bush grasshopper. All crickets and grasshoppers have long, strong back legs. They're great for doing the high jump! Their legs have another, more unusual, use, too. Some grasshoppers and crickets rub their legs against their bodies to make their noisy chirping songs.

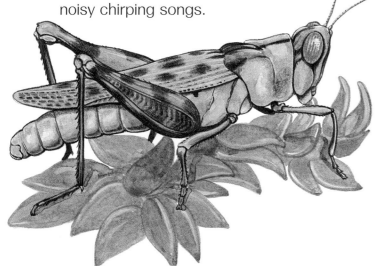

Which minibeast has lots of legs?

Millipedes have more legs than most other minibeasts. The name millipede means "thousand-legged." But even this giant millipede does not have that many! Most millipedes have between 100 and 400 legs. They have four legs on each part, or segment, of their bodies. Even though millipedes have lots of legs, they move quite slowly. They walk by lifting up groups of legs at a time. Some legs are swinging forward while others are moving backward. Each foot touches the ground just before the one in front in a wavelike movement.

How do worms move without legs?

An earthworm's body is divided into tiny sections, called segments. Each segment has special hairs to help the worm grip the soil. At rest, a worm's segments are all the same size.

1. To move forward, the hairs on the worm's back end grip the soil. Then the worm stretches its front end forward as far as it can go. These front segments become long and thin.

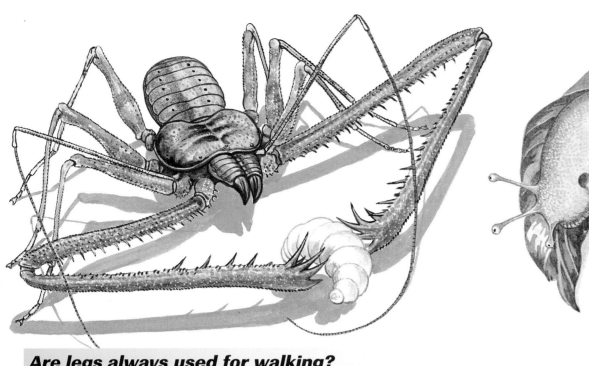

Are legs always used for walking?

Like all scorpions, the tail-less whip scorpion has eight legs. But only six are used for walking. The long front legs are used as feelers. The scorpion uses them to feel its way around in the dark. When the scorpion finds a tasty meal, it grabs its prey with its huge spiny claws.

How do slugs move?

Snails and slugs, like this orange-colored great black slug, belong to a group of animals called mollusks. They do not have legs for walking, but they do have a foot! This foot is the flat, slimy base of the animal's body. It is made up of one big muscle. Wavelike ripples pass down the foot muscle from front to back. These movements pull the slug forward over a trail of slippery slime.

Do centipedes have 100 legs?

Centipedes can have between 30 and 354 legs. They have one pair of legs for each part, or segment, of their bodies. Unlike plant-eating millipedes, centipedes are fierce hunters. This cave centipede uses its long legs to race after its prey. It also uses them to feel its way around the dark caves where it lives. A centipede can even bite with its clawlike front legs!

2. Next, the worm stops stretching, and the front section thickens again. The back hairs unhook, and the front hairs grip the soil. The next section then stretches, pulling the back end forward.

3. The earthworm repeats these actions. It stretches and thickens each section of its body in turn. As it stretches and thickens the worm moves forward.

Color Codes

Many creepy crawlies are hard to see. The hunters and the hunted both use tricks to help them hide. Some bugs blend in with their background or look like other objects. This is called camouflage. Creepy crawlies are often brightly colored, too. Some use their colors to attract a mate. Other bright bugs match the color of their surroundings. For some minibeasts, bright colors act as a warning. They may have stings or venom (poison), or they may taste awful. Their patterns and markings warn "Keep clear. I'm dangerous."

Are red bugs dangerous?

People often use the color red as a danger signal and so do other animals. Many bugs, like the red-spotted ladybug, use bright, strong colors to warn other animals that they taste nasty. A hunter may try to eat one, but it soon finds that it makes a horrible-tasting meal. The hunter soon learns not to catch such brightly colored bugs again!

Why are some bugs strange shapes?

Some bugs, like this African devil mantis, are shaped to help them hide among plants. This insect looks like the petals, leaves, and stems of a plant. The mantis is also brightly colored to match the flowers and leaves of the plant that it lives on. It blends in so well that other insects—its prey—do not see it hiding there. This helps the mantis, which is a fierce hunter. As an insect passes by, the mantis grabs it in its spiny front legs.

Do creepy crawlies talk to each other?

Creepy crawlies don't really talk, but they do send signals. The bush cricket sings by rubbing its wings together. Male crickets sing to get a female's attention.

Fireflies need to be able to find each other as they fly through the dark night sky. To do this they flash their lights at one another. Different species have different flash patterns!

12

The hoverfly looks like a wasp but it hasn't got a sting. Many animals are fooled by the hoverfly's stripes and keep away. Copying colors and patterns in this way is called mimicry and it can be a means of protection. You can tell a hoverfly from a wasp by the way it flies. A hoverfly darts about and hovers in midair like a mini-helicopter.

Why are wasps black and yellow?

The bold yellow and black stripes of this common wasp are easy to see. They give other animals a clear warning: "Stay away! Or I'll sting you!" Other creatures know that these colors mean danger. So they keep out of the wasp's way. That's what you should do, too. Leave wasps and bees alone and they will soon buzz off back to their nests.

Are all butterflies brightly colored?

No, some butterflies are white or pale colored. But many butterflies do use bright colors to attract a mate. This blue morpho butterfly lives in tropical forests where there is little light. When they are ready to mate, groups of blue morphos gather in forest clearings. Their brilliant colors glow as they flit and dance in shafts of bright sunlight.

Some bugs use vibration signals to talk to each other. A male field spider visiting a female can tug a thread of her web to tell her he's there. She can send a message back by tugging her end!

Bugs may need to give each other messages when they are near one another, too. One way an ant can talk to another ant is by tapping the other ant with its antennae.

13

Feeding Time

All animals need to eat to stay alive. Most minibeasts have mouths for eating and drinking. They don't have teeth in their mouths like you, but they do have mouthparts. The way a bug's mouthparts look and work depends on the food it eats. Some creepy crawlies have sharp, cutting mouthparts for biting and tearing up their food. Others have sucking or needlelike mouthparts to drink a liquid meal. Some bugs are hunters, catching and killing other animals for their food. Others feed on plants.

Proboscis coiled for flying

Proboscis uncoiled for feeding

What do butterflies eat?

Butterflies, such as this red admiral, drink nectar from flowers. A butterfly's mouthparts are shaped like a drinking straw. They are called a proboscis. It sucks up the thick, sugary liquid through the hollow tube, just like you suck up a milk shake. When a butterfly is not feeding, its proboscis is coiled up under its head. Moths feed in the same way.

Do spiders have teeth?

Spiders have two sharp fangs to stab and kill their prey. The trap-door spider's fangs are huge, black and shiny. The fangs are fixed to a short, furry part of the mouth. A hole leads from the mouth to each fang. When a spider catches its prey, it stabs it with its fangs. Venom flows through the holes into the fangs and is injected into the prey. Juices in the venom break down the body of the victim. Most spiders then suck up their food, like sucking thick soup through a straw.

Fangs

How do spiders catch their food?

Many spiders make webs of silk to catch their prey.
1. First, the spider fastens one end of its silk to a twig. Then it lets the breeze blow the silk onto another twig to make a bridge.

2. The spider makes a loop of silk below the bridge. From the middle of the loop it spins a shorter loop and drops to form a "Y" shape. At the bottom, the spider fastens the silk.

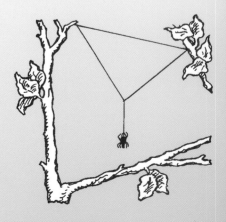

How do flies feed?

Flies, such as the bluebottle, have mouthparts shaped like a sponge on a stalk. When a fly lands on food, it drips juices from its mouth onto the food. These juices break the food down into a thin, runny liquid. Then the fly uses its spongy mouthparts to mop up its soupy food.

Can beetles eat wood?

Even though wood is tough, some minibeasts, like the death watch beetle, make a meal of it. This beetle has mouthparts like powerful pincers. Its strong jaws move these pincers from side to side to shred the wood into bits. The beetle bores through the solid wood until it comes out of a small hole. The male also uses its strong jaws to tap on the wood to attract a mate.

Do bugs eat plants?

Lots of creepy crawlies feed on the leaves, stems, flowers, and roots of plants. Many bugs, like these aphids, feed on plant sap. Sap is a sweet liquid, full of goodness. It runs through tiny tubes inside a plant's stems, stalks, and leaves. The aphid pierces the plant with its hollow, needlelike mouthparts and sucks up the sap.

3. Next, the spider goes back to the center of the web. It spins several more lines to make a framework between the twigs and leaves. These strands are made of nonsticky silk.

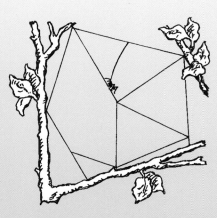

4. The spider spins more threads out from the center like the spokes of a wheel. Then it spins a spiral of sticky threads around the web. This sticky spiral will catch small animals.

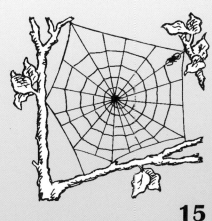

Biting Bugs

Most creepy crawlies either eat other animals or are themselves eaten. So it is not surprising that they have developed many ways of killing prey and defending themselves. Some, such as bees, wasps, and hornets, have nasty stings in their tails. Others, like spiders and ants, have beastly bites. Some creepy crawlies even have deadly venoms to make up for their tiny size. Many bugs sting or bite if they think they are in danger. Others sting or bite to kill their food or keep it quiet while they eat it!

Can scorpions hurt you?

Yes, if they sting you! Scorpions, like this green scorpion, have a sharp sting at the end of their tails. They use their sting to inject venom into their prey to stop it moving. They also sting other animals if they come too close. Some scorpions' venom is strong enough to kill a person. If you see a scorpion, it's wise to stay away.

Why can bees only sting once?

A bee's sting is not smooth like a wasp's sting. It has a backward-pointing barb. So, when a bee stings, it can't pull its sting out again. The sting, with its bag of venom, is ripped from the rear end of the bee's body. The bee soon dies. These bumblebees sting to protect themselves or their nest. Their bright yellow and black stripes act as a warning to this mouse which will quickly run away!

Are bugs poisonous?

Yes, some bugs have poisons in their bodies. Many get the poison from their food. Milkweed bugs eat poisonous seed pods. If you ate this food it would make you sick.

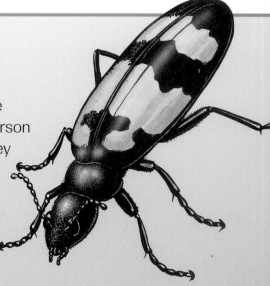

Blister beetles produce a burning liquid. If a person touches this poison they can get a nasty blister. If an animal swallows this liquid it can cause their insides to burn.

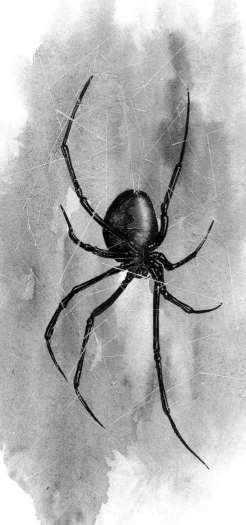

Do spiders bite?

Spiders have sharp fangs and many can give a venomous bite. Not many spiders have fangs strong enough to cut human skin. But some, like this black widow spider, have venom strong enough to kill you. A spider usually uses its venom to catch food. It stabs its prey with its fangs and injects the venom. The victim is alive but it cannot move, and the spider can eat it.

Do some bugs drink blood?

Yes, some bugs, like this mosquito, feed on blood. The mosquito is a kind of fly with a hollow, needlelike mouth. It pushes its sharp mouthparts through your skin, then sucks up your blood. Its saliva (spit) keeps your blood runny while it feeds. This saliva also causes the itchy red lump you get after a mosquito bite.

Can stag beetles bite you?

No, a stag beetle's jaws may look scary but they're not strong enough to bite you. Only male beetles have the huge antler-shaped jaws. They are just for show and for fighting other males. Male stag beetles lock jaws and push and shove one another to try to win a battle for a female.

Monarch butterflies and caterpillars are poisonous to many other animals. When eaten, the poison makes the hunter's heart beat very fast and it makes breathing very difficult.

Tiger moths can be deadly dangerous. But, at dawn and dusk, they use a special warning signal. They make a high, squeaky sound to tell hunters that they are not a tasty treat!

17

Living Together

Some creepy crawlies, such as termites, ants, and bees, live together in large groups called colonies. All the animals in the group help one another collect food, find shelter, and fight enemies. This helps the whole group survive. Insects that live in colonies are called social insects. Bugs that don't usually live in groups sometimes gather together for other reasons. This may be to mate, or at a good feeding place. They will soon go off on their own again.

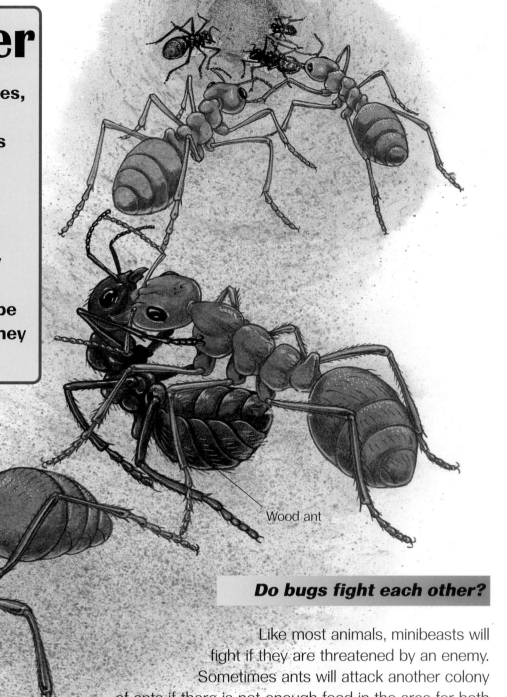

Amazon ant

Wood ant

Wood ant larva

Do bugs fight each other?

Like most animals, minibeasts will fight if they are threatened by an enemy. Sometimes ants will attack another colony of ants if there is not enough food in the area for both groups. These Amazon ants are attacking a nearby nest of wood ants. The Amazon ants will take away the wood ants' eggs and young. They may eat them or raise the young wood ants as slaves. The Amazon ants may also set up their own colony in the wood ants' nest.

Why do bees dance?

1. A honeybee dances to tell other bees where she has found food. If the food is within 55 yards, the scout bee dances in a circle, then turns and circles in the other direction.

2. When flowers are farther away, the scout dances a figure eight. Facing downward on the honeycomb means the food is on the other side of the hive from the sun.

How big are bees' nests?

Bees' nests vary in size depending on the kind of bee. These honeybees live together in large nests of up to 50,000 bees. There are three types of honeybee, all with different jobs in the hive. The queen bee spends her time laying eggs—up to 1,500 a day. Worker bees look after the hive, the queen, and the young. They also gather nectar and make honey. Males, called drones, mate with the queen. Beekeepers build special hives for honeybees so they can remove the honey easily.

Do some bees live alone?

Many kinds of bees and wasps live on their own. They build small nests in the ground or in hollow plant stems. The female potter wasp mixes sand and mud with her saliva to make a vase-shaped nest. She stings a caterpillar to paralyze it and places it in the nest. Then she lays her eggs on it. Her larvae will have a ready-made meal when they hatch.

Why do bugs all live in the same place?

Most minibeasts, such as these woodlice, live on their own. They gather together by chance because they live in the same kinds of places. Woodlice need to live in damp places, such as under leaves or the bark of a tree. They must not dry out, or they will die. That is why you often find several living in the same damp place.

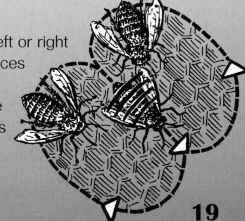

3. If the flowers are between the sun and the hive, the scout dances up the hive wall. Dancing in a straight line slowly means the food is far away. If she moves fast, the food is nearby.

4. If the food is to the left or right of the hive, the bee dances at an angle in the same direction. The angle she dances tells the workers the angle between the flowers and the sun.

Baby Bugs

Most large animals, such as humans, only have a few babies. Minibeasts produce hundreds and thousands of young in their lifetime. Most female creepy crawlies lay hundreds of eggs at a time. Lots of baby and adult bugs get eaten by other animals. Producing lots of babies increases the chance that some of them will not be eaten. The young bugs that survive will grow up and have their own babies.

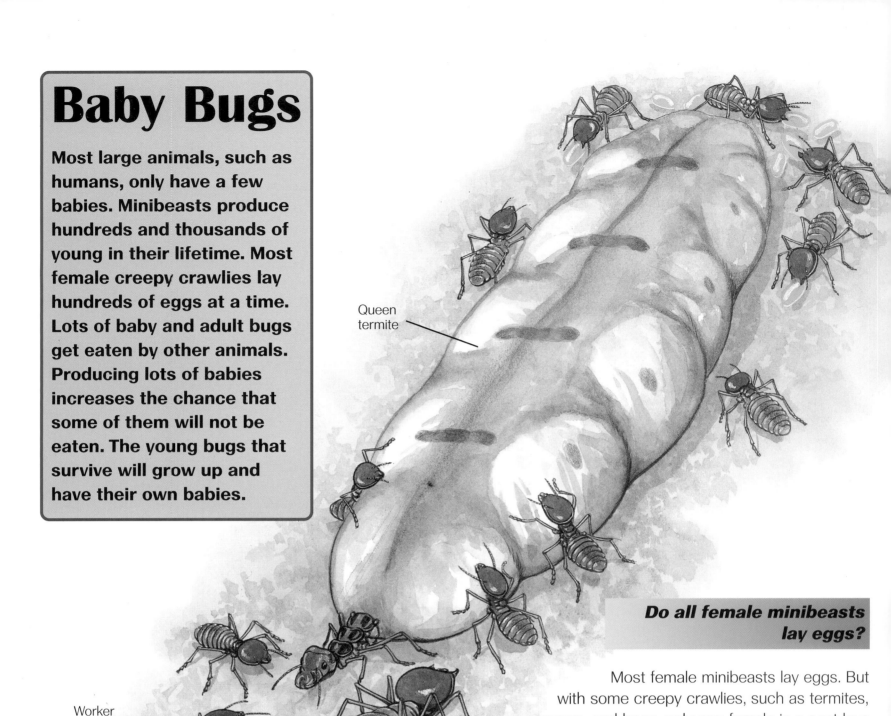

Queen termite

Worker termite

King termite

Do all female minibeasts lay eggs?

Most female minibeasts lay eggs. But with some creepy crawlies, such as termites, wasps, and bees, only one female in a nest lays eggs. The queen termite is the only termite to produce young. Her swollen body is a huge egg-laying machine. She may lay as many as four million eggs a year. Her mate is the king termite. The queen is looked after by a team of worker termites. They feed her, clean her, and clear up her droppings. Other teams of workers look after the eggs and baby termites.

How do wasps build nests?

1. The queen wasp starts the work. First, she finds a good spot in a tree or in the roof of a house. She uses "paper" made from chewed-up wood to build a bowl-shaped shelter.

2. Next, she makes a narrow stalk with a small cap. Inside the cap are three to seven six-sided cells that fit together. The queen lays an egg in each one. Then she builds the nest walls.

Do creepy crawlies guard their young?

Most creepy crawlies do not look after their eggs or young. That is why so many of them get eaten. But bull ants make sure that no one eats their young. Worker bull ants guard the eggs and larvae. The workers have big, strong, biting mouthparts. If an enemy enters the nest, the workers attack it. They squirt the creature with stinging acid and bite it with their giant jaws.

Do insects look after their babies?

Most insects do not look after their young. The females lay their eggs and then leave the young to hatch on their own. Male insects often do even less! This is not true of the giant water bug from North America. The female glues her eggs to the male's folded wings. He carries the eggs on his back until they hatch.

Where do bugs lay their eggs?

Most female bugs lay hundreds of eggs at a time. But they usually lay them in special places. Some, like the female cockroach, hide them in a crack or crevice. Ants build nests. Flies and moths lay their eggs on food for the baby larvae. The female window-winged moth sticks hers to a blade of grass. When the caterpillars hatch, they can start to munch right away!

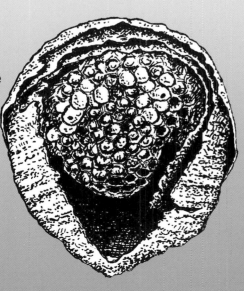

3. The queen builds up the nest walls from layers of paper to make a ball shape. The queen's eggs hatch into larvae, which grow into female workers. These help build the nest.

4. The workers collect wood and chew it to a pulp. Then they spit it out to make more cells. The queen lays an egg in each new cell. There can be up to 5,000 wasps in a nest!

Bloodsuckers

Minibeasts can live almost anywhere. Some are parasites. They make their homes on, or in, other animals, including humans! A parasite is an animal that gets food and shelter from another animal, called a host. Some parasites live on the host and suck its blood. Others live inside the host's body. Some, such as mites, burrow into the skin. Others live in the blood or gut, where there is a ready supply of food. Many parasites harm their hosts. Some spread nasty diseases, while others can make people ill or even kill them.

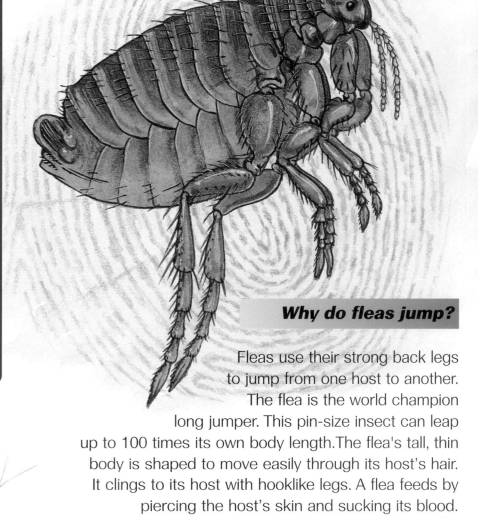

Why do fleas jump?

Fleas use their strong back legs to jump from one host to another. The flea is the world champion long jumper. This pin-size insect can leap up to 100 times its own body length. The flea's tall, thin body is shaped to move easily through its host's hair. It clings to its host with hooklike legs. A flea feeds by piercing the host's skin and sucking its blood.

Can ticks harm you?

Yes, a tick can spread germs when it bites you and sucks your blood. These tiny eight-legged creatures belong to the same group of animals as spiders. The hard tick lives on animals such as sheep and cattle as well as people. It can carry disease from one host to another. The tick clings to the skin of its host by its mouthparts. It can swell to seven times its normal size after a long drink of blood!

Do people ever eat bugs?

Yes, some bugs are full of goodness, but others are poisonous. Australian Aboriginals like to eat witchetty grubs. These fat white grubs are eaten raw or cooked.

Honey pot ants store a sweet food called honeydew in their abdomens. People dig up these tasty ants. Then they bite off the ant's abdomen and swallow!

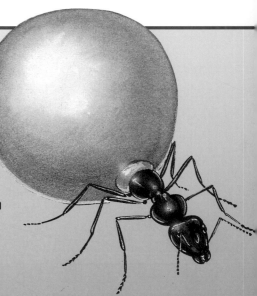

Why do some bugs drink blood?

Bugs, such as the benchuca bug from South America, drink blood because it is a good food. This bug stabs a person with its sharp mouthparts and sucks up the blood. Then it flies off to feed on another person. It does not drink enough blood to harm its victims, but it can spread disease. This bug has parasites in its gut that can also make people ill. The parasites are carried into the wound made by the bug as it feeds.

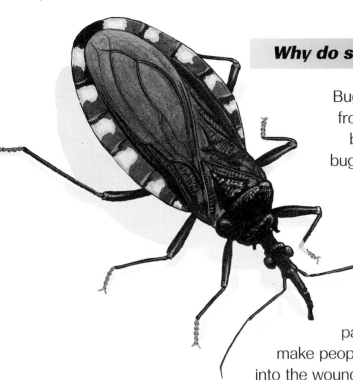

Eggs (nits)

Adult louse

Do bugs really live in beds?

Yes, tiny bed bugs live in furniture, especially beds and carpets. At night they come out to feed on human blood. Bed bugs have long tubelike snouts. They use them to pierce your skin and suck up your blood. Their bites can cause itchy sores.

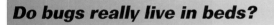

What are nits?

Nits are the eggs of bloodsucking human head lice. An adult louse clings to people's hair with its hook-shaped legs. The lice can crawl from one person's head to another if the heads get close enough to touch. The louse feeds by sucking blood from your scalp. The female louse lays lots of eggs. She glues them to hairs to keep them safe. The eggs hatch in about seven days and the young start to feed.

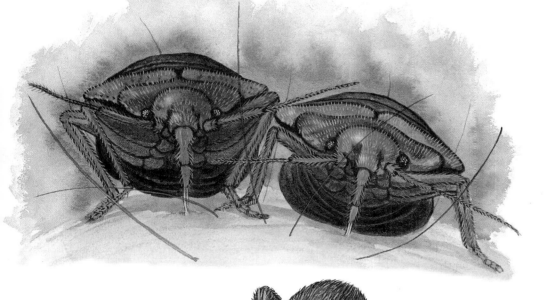

Some people like to eat spiders. Edible tarantulas live in the forests of Southeast Asia. Local people kill them and cook them over an open fire to burn off the stinging hairs.

Palolo worms look like green spaghetti. They live in dead coral reefs in the Pacific Ocean. In Samoa and Fiji people catch the worms in nets. They eat them lightly fried or raw!

Water Bugs

Creepy crawlies live all over the world. They are found in forests, up mountains, in the desert, underground, and under the water. Thousands of different kinds of minibeasts live in streams, ponds, and lakes. Some even live in the ocean. Most creepy crawlies breathe air, so living under the water can be a problem. Many do not have the special body parts, called gills, that let them breathe in water. Instead, they have to swim to the surface for a regular supply of air. Some store this air as tiny bubbles around their bodies.

How do bugs swim?

Many insects, like this great diving beetle, use their legs to row through the water. The diving beetle is a strong swimmer, chasing after its prey of small fish and tadpoles. It keeps a store of air trapped beneath its hard wing cases. On land, it can run like any other beetle and has wings for flying.

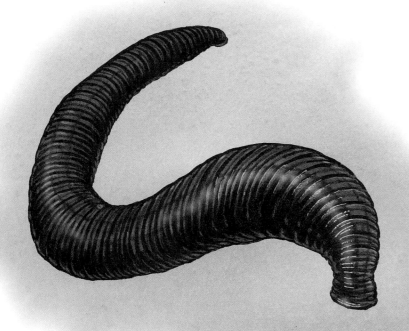

Do earthworms live in water?

Earthworms cannot live in water. But a relative of the earthworm—the leech—lives in water or damp places on land. The leech is a parasite. It uses the suckers at each end of its body to stick onto a larger animal. Then it bites the animal with its jagged jaws and sucks its blood. The medicinal leech can drink five times its own weight at one feeding. In the past, doctors tried to cure sick people by using leeches to drain off their blood.

Which spider builds a diving bell?

1. The water spider lives under the water by building a diving bell of silk. It can also breathe when it dives under the water by using bubbles of air trapped in the hairs on its body.

2. The spider swims and crawls among the weeds. To begin building, the spider spins a platform of silk between the plant stems. Then it builds a bell-shaped web.

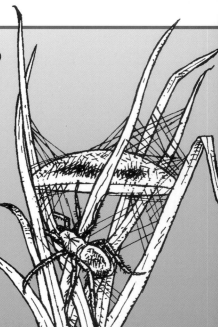

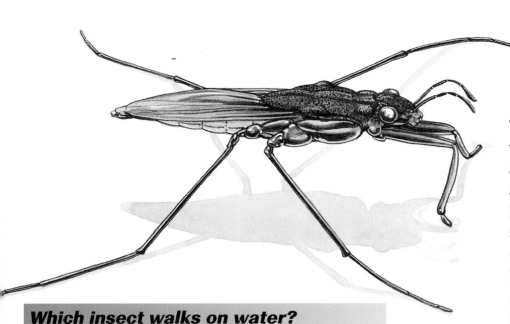

Which insect walks on water?

The pond skater can skim across water at speed. This tiny insect is held up by the "skin" on the top of the water. This "skin" is called surface tension. The pond skater is a hunter. It slides across the water to catch small creatures trapped in the surface "skin." It spears its victim with needle-sharp mouthparts. Then it sucks the juices from the animal's body.

Can insects live in fast-flowing water?

Most water bugs live in still water, such as ponds or lakes. The current in fast-flowing water could wash them away or crush them. But the stonefly nymph has found a way to stay still in rushing streams. It uses its strong, splayed-out legs and hooked feet to cling to stones on the stream bed.

Which insect has a snorkel?

When you swim under the water, you can use a snorkel to breathe air. The water scorpion also uses a kind of snorkel. Its breathing tube is on its tail, so its whole body stays under the water. It is hard to see among the pond weeds. Its brown body hangs beneath the water like a dead leaf. When a bug or tadpole passes, the water scorpion strikes. It grabs its prey in pincerlike front legs, then chews it up.

Do bugs like dirty water?

Most water bugs can only live in fresh water. But the larva of the drone fly likes living in mud or dirty water. It feeds on rotten plants until it is fully grown. It has a long breathing tube. This tube is so long that it looks like the tail of a rat. This is why it's also called the rat-tailed maggot!

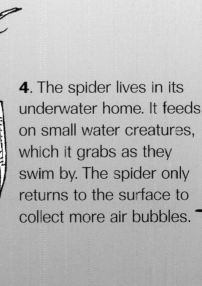

3. When the spider has completed this, it swims to the surface to collect air to fill the web. The silk is closely woven so that it is waterproof. The air stays trapped inside.

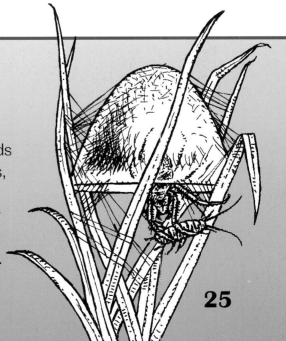

4. The spider lives in its underwater home. It feeds on small water creatures, which it grabs as they swim by. The spider only returns to the surface to collect more air bubbles.

Bug Pests

Some people are afraid of creepy crawlies, especially spiders. Often there is no good reason as the creatures are harmless. With other minibeasts, it is wise to be careful. Some bugs are pests, causing harm or damage to crops and plants. Others can make farm animals and pets ill. Some bugs spread germs or diseases in humans. Others may bite, sting, or poison you. Minibeasts can burrow into wood and destroy your homes. They will even eat your clothes!

Do bugs eat our food?

Yes, many bugs eat the same plants that we do. Some, such as Colorado beetles, can cause a lot of damage. The black-and-yellow adults feed on potato leaves. So do their orange-red larvae. They can destroy huge fields of potatoes in a few days. People are asked to tell farmers if they see this beetle. Then the farmers can use special sprays to kill them.

Why don't people like spiders?

Not everyone hates spiders. Some people like them and keep them as pets. People often find big hairy spiders, like tarantulas, scary. But many of them are harmless. Some can give you a nasty bite, but they hardly ever kill people. Often small spiders are far more dangerous. Australian redbacks and funnel webs and North American black widow spiders are much more deadly.

Are some bugs our friends?

Yes, some creepy crawlies are useful little helpers. The wolf spider helps people by hunting and eating caterpillars that can do serious damage to crops.

People may be scared of being stung by bees, but bees also provide us with a sweet treat—honey! They also give us beeswax, which is used to make furniture polish.

Minibeasts sometimes gather together in swarms to mate. At other times it is to find more food or space. Huge swarms of locusts build up every few years in parts of Africa and Asia. Hundreds of them fly a long way to find food. They eat all the food in an area, then move on. The locusts breed as they go and the swarm grows. Locust nymphs are called hoppers. They have small wings and cannot fly. But they can eat! They eat everything in their path. Sometimes they eat all the food crops in a region and thousands of people starve.

Can harmless bugs make you ill?

Yes, some harmless bugs can hurt you by spreading diseases. In Africa, a disease called sleeping sickness, or nagana, is spread by the tsetse fly. The fly bites an animal or person that has the disease. As the fly sucks their blood, it takes in the germs. Then the tsetse fly flies off to its next victim. The fly "injects" the animal with the harmful germs as it bites it.

Do bugs eat clothes?

Yes, the caterpillars of clothes moths will make a meal of your gloves. Or any other clothes they can find! The caterpillars change into pupae and then into adult moths. The adults lay their eggs on your clothes. The eggs hatch into caterpillars—and so the cycle starts again.

Snails are a nuisance to gardeners—they like to eat plants. Luckily for us, ground beetles like to eat snails!

The silk moth is a very special bug. The caterpillar of this moth spins a fine silken thread to make its cocoon. People collect this thread to make silk fabric.

27

What do you know about creepy crawlies?

1 **Which bug will die if it stings you?**
a) scorpion
b) wasp
c) bee

2 **Which colorful bug only pretends to be nasty?**
a) Colorado beetle
b) hoverfly
c) blister beetle

3 **What is the "juice" of plants called?**
a) milk
b) sap
c) honey

4 **How many legs does a millipede have?**
a) between 1,000 and 4,000
b) between 100 and 400
c) between 10 and 40

5 **Which bug likes to eat wood?**
a) red admiral butterfly
b) bush cricket
c) death watch beetle

6 **Which of these creepy crawlies builds a nest?**
a) ant
b) cockroach
c) butterfly

7 **How many honeybees can live in one nest?**
a) 500
b) 5,000
c) 50,000

8 **What do you call a large group of insects who live together?**
a) a family
b) a colony
c) a school

9 **What is it called when an insect changes its body shape?**
a) camouflage
b) getting dressed
c) metamorphosis

10 **What is another name for a butterfly or moth pupa?**
a) caterpillar
b) larva
c) chrysalis

11 **Which of these scorpions no longer exists?**
a) *Gigantoscorpion*
b) water scorpion
c) green scorpion

12 **What is another name for the eggs of head lice?**
a) ticks
b) fleas
c) nits

13 **Which of these scary spiders are often kept as pets?**
a) funnel web
b) tarantula
c) black widow

14 **Why do mosquitoes bite people?**
a) to eat their skin
b) to drink their blood
c) to scare them away

15 **Which of these bugs uses bright colors to camouflage itself?**
a) bumblebee
b) blue morpho butterfly
c) African devil mantis

16 **What are antennae used for?**
a) feeling and smelling
b) biting and stinging
c) eating and drinking

17 **Which creepy crawlies sing by rubbing their legs together?**
a) centipedes
b) grasshoppers
c) stag beetles

18 **Which type of ant do some people like to eat?**
a) bull ants
b) Amazon ants
c) honey pot ants

19 **What is the name for baby bugs that look like mini-adults?**
a) maggots
b) nymphs
c) larvae

20 **Which bug can spread disease?**
a) tsetse fly
b) clothes moth
c) locusts

21 **What are midges?**
a) tiny beetles
b) tiny worms
c) tiny flies

22 **Which bugs did doctors once use to try to cure sick people?**
a) earthworms
b) leeches
c) benchuca bugs

23 **Which bug likes to eat potato plants?**
a) Colorado beetle
b) giant African land snail
c) giant Australian earthworm

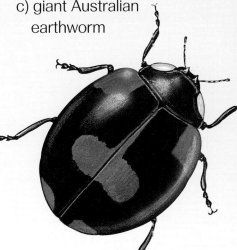

24 **Which is one of the smallest creepy crawlies?**
a) Goliath beetle
b) fairy fly wasp
c) redback spider

Index

Answers to Quiz

1	c) bee	7	c) 50,000	16	a) feeling and smelling
2	b) hoverfly	8	b) a colony	17	b) grasshoppers
3	b) sap	9	c) metamorphosis	18	c) honey pot ants
4	b) between 100 and 400	10	c) chrysalis	19	b) nymphs
5	c) death watch beetle	11	a) *Gigantoscorpion*	20	a) tsetse fly
6	a) ant	12	c) nits	21	c) tiny flies
		13	b) tarantula	22	b) leeches
		14	b) to drink their blood	23	a) Colorado beetle
		15	c) African devil mantis	24	b) fairy fly wasp